A Robbie Reader

Meet Our New Student From

NIGERIA

Anna M. Ogunnaike

P.O. Box 196
Hockessin, Delaware 19707
Visit us on the web: www.mitchelllane.com
Comments? email us: mitchelllane@mitchelllane.com

Meet Our New Student From

Australia • China • Colombia • Great Britain
• Haiti • India • Israel • Japan • Korea • Malaysia •
Mali • Mexico • New Zealand • Nicaragua • **Nigeria**
• Quebec • South Africa • Tanzania • Zambia •
Going to School Around the World

ABOUT THE COVER: Abeokuta is a city of 200,000 people in Ogun State. Abeokuta is the birthplace of many famous Nigerians, including past president of Nigeria Olusegun Obasanjo, and Nobel Prize–winning author Wole Soyinka.

PUBLISHER'S NOTE: The facts on which the story in this book is based have been thoroughly researched. Documentation of such research can be found on page 44. While every possible effort has been made to ensure accuracy, the publisher will not assume liability for damages caused by inaccuracies in the data, and makes no warranty on the accuracy of the information contained herein.

To reflect current usage, we have chosen to use the secular era designations BCE ("before the common era") and CE ("of the common era") instead of the traditional designations BC ("before Christ") and AD (*anno Domini*, "in the year of the Lord").

Library of Congress Cataloging-in-Publication Data

Ogunnaike, Anna M.
  Meet our new student from Nigeria / by Anna M. Ogunnaike.
     p. cm. — (A Robbie reader)
  Includes bibliographical references and index.
  ISBN 978-1-58415-655-0 (library bound)
  1. Nigeria—Juvenile literature. I. Title.
  DT515.22.O44 2008
  966.9—dc22

                                        2008007904

Printing   2   3   4   5   6   7   8   9

                                 PLB / PLB2

CONTENTS

Nigeria

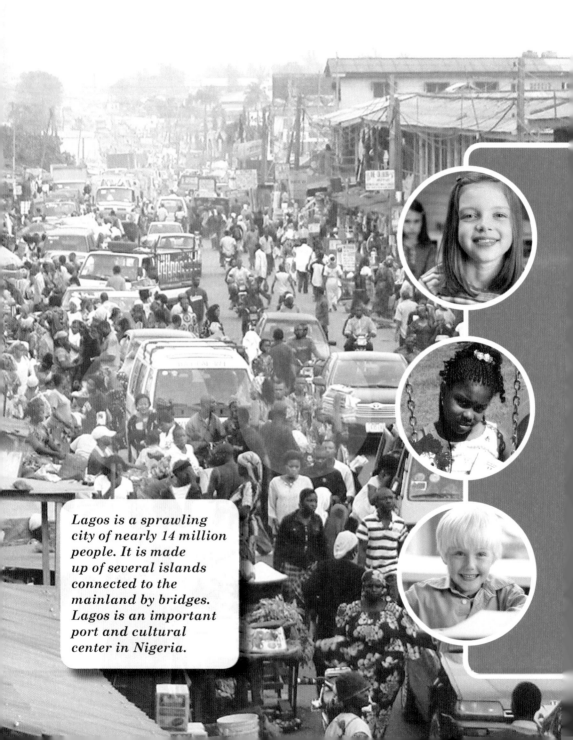

Lagos is a sprawling city of nearly 14 million people. It is made up of several islands connected to the mainland by bridges. Lagos is an important port and cultural center in Nigeria.

A New Classmate

Chapter

Julie was so excited! Mrs. Harkins had just announced that a new student from Nigeria would be joining their third-grade class. Julie had never met anyone from the continent of Africa. She had so many questions she wanted to ask about the new student and about Nigeria.

Julie raised her hand. "Mrs. Harkins, what's the new student's name?" she asked.

"Our new student's name is Mayowa Adewale, Julie," Mrs. Harkins answered. She said her name MAH-yoh-wah ah-DAY-wah-lay. "She's eight years old and is moving here from the city of Lagos. She will join our class next week. I would like us to learn all we can about Nigeria before Mayowa's arrival so that we can make her feel welcome. Let's begin by finding Nigeria on the world map."

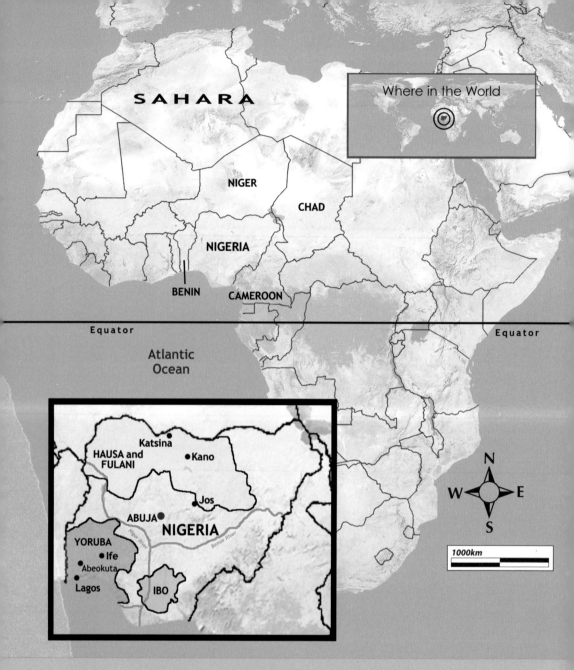

FACTS ABOUT THE FEDERAL REPUBLIC OF NIGERIA

Nigeria Total Area:
356,670 square miles
(923,768 square kilometers)

Population:
135,031,000 (2007 estimate)

Capital City:
Abuja

Monetary Unit:
Naira

Religions:
Islam, Christianity,
and local religions

Languages:
English (official); Hausa; Yoruba;
Ibo (Igbo); Fulani

Chief Exports:
Petroleum and petroleum
products (oil), cocoa, rubber

Mrs. Harkins helped Julie and her classmates find the continent of Africa on the world map, and then pointed to the large bulge of West Africa. "Follow the coast of West Africa until it turns sharply to the south, just above the **equator**. There you will see the country of Nigeria."

"If Nigeria is near the equator, then it must be very hot there," said Julie.

"Do elephants and giraffes live in Nigeria?" Eric asked.

"Yes, Eric, but not many large animals live in the wild in Nigeria any longer. Most of these animals now live in game reserves," answered Mrs. Harkins.

The city of Lagos has skyscrapers and a lively business district. It is also known for its popular music and film industries.

The Yankari National Park in Bauchi State is home to elephants, lions, hyenas, hippopotamuses, baboons, monkeys, and antelope. Over 350 different species of birds also live in the park.

Julie wondered what Mayowa's house in Lagos looked like. Then she thought of another important question. "Mrs. Harkins, does Mayowa speak English?"

"Yes, Julie," said Mrs. Harkins. "Nigeria was once a **colony** of Great Britain, and the official language of Nigeria is English. However, most Nigerians speak a local Nigerian language in addition to English. Good questions, class! Your homework for this evening will

Giraffes are the tallest land mammals on earth. Their long necks make it possible for them to eat the leaves from the top of the thorny acacia tree. A type of giraffe called the Nigerian giraffe has become quite rare.

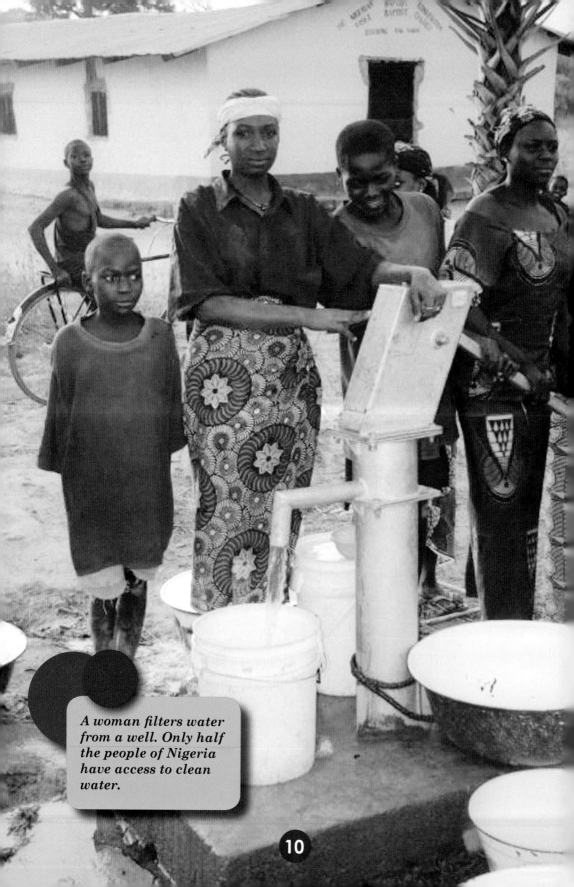

A woman filters water from a well. Only half the people of Nigeria have access to clean water.

The flag of the Colony and Protectorate of Nigeria, which was formed in 1914. Under British rule, Nigerians were not allowed to vote, but were forced to pay taxes to the British government.

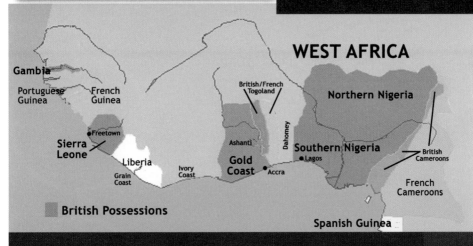

WEST AFRICA

Gambia

Portuguese Guinea

French Guinea

British/French Togoland

Northern Nigeria

Freetown

Sierra Leone

Ashanti

Dahomey

Southern Nigeria

British Cameroons

Liberia

Ivory Coast

Gold Coast

Accra

Lagos

Grain Coast

French Cameroons

British Possessions

Spanish Guinea

Great Britain colonized Nigeria and many other parts of Africa in the late 1800s. Most African nations gained independence in the 1960s.

be to learn at least three facts about Nigeria and be prepared to share what you have learned with the class tomorrow. Then we will plan a special party to welcome Mayowa."

The class buzzed with excitement. Before she left for home, Julie stopped in the school library to look for a book about Nigeria. She wondered what questions Mayowa had about the United States, and if Mayowa was nervous about moving to a new country.

The oldest civilization in West Africa is known as the Nok civilization. In the early 1900s, tin miners discovered ancient terra-cotta statues made by the Nok people. Archaeologists (ar-kee-AH-luh-jists) believe that the Nok civilization existed in the central part of present-day Nigeria from about 500 to 200 BCE.

The Giant of Africa

Chapter 2

Nigeria is known as the "giant of Africa" because it is the most **populous** country in Africa. By 2008, over 135 million people were living in Nigeria, and one out of every four Africans was a Nigerian. Nigeria is also very diverse. There are at least 250 different ethnic groups in Nigeria, each with its own language, history, and culture. The largest ethnic groups in Nigeria are the Hausa, Fulani, Yoruba, and Ibo (or Igbo) peoples.

Long before the arrival of Europeans in Africa, rich and powerful **civilizations** existed in West Africa. During the Middle Ages (around 500 to 1450 CE), Africans established the Oyo, Benin, and Kanem-Bornu kingdoms in the land today known as Nigeria.

The Hausa people settled in the northern part of what is now Nigeria around 900 CE. They set up powerful **city-states** such as Kano. These cities were and still are important centers of trade. **Caravans** crossed the

Sahara on camels from North Africa, bringing glass and salt to trade for **ivory**, **ebony**, gold, and slaves. The Fulani people, **nomadic** herders who raised cattle and sheep, also settled in this region. In the 1300s, Arab traders introduced the religion of **Islam** to the Hausa and Fulani people.

In the southwestern region of Nigeria, the Yoruba people built the city of Ife (pronounced EE-feh) around the year 500 BCE. According to Yoruba tradition, Ife was where the supreme god, *Olodamare* (oh-LOH-duh-mah-ray), created the first human beings out of clay. The craftsmen of Ife were famous for the **terra-cotta** sculptures and bronze castings they made. The Yoruba built cities that were ruled by an *oba* (king).

The Ibo people settled in the southeastern region of Nigeria in the 800s. Unlike the Yoruba and the Hausa, the Ibo people had no kings or central rulers. They lived in villages, and a council (group) of elders made decisions for the community.

Portuguese traders were the first Europeans to visit West Africa. By the late 1400s, the Portuguese were trading cloth, beads, and copper for gold, ivory, and slaves. In the period between the late 1400s and the early 1800s, about 12 million West Africans were sold into slavery. They were taken in ships to work on **plantations** in North and South America. The southern coast of present-day Nigeria became known as the Slave Coast. Slavery was not new to West Africa, as

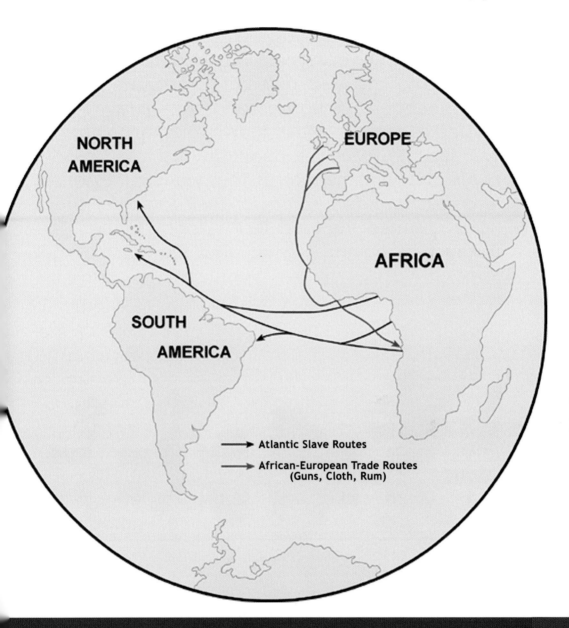

NORTH AMERICA

EUROPE

AFRICA

SOUTH AMERICA

→ Atlantic Slave Routes

→ African-European Trade Routes
(Guns, Cloth, Rum)

The journey from Africa to the American colonies was known as the Middle Passage. Captured Africans were chained together and placed on wooden planks in the holds of ships. Many Africans died of sickness or starvation during the long sea voyage.

African prisoners of war were sometimes kept as servants. However, slavery as practiced by the Europeans was very different. Captured Africans found themselves living thousands of miles from home, treated as property rather than as human beings.

In the late 1800s, Europeans divided the continent of Africa among themselves. They wanted the natural resources found in Africa for their factories. Great Britain claimed the land that is today Nigeria. The colony was named Nigeria after the mighty Niger River.

The Niger River is the third longest river in Africa. It is over 2,500 miles long. It begins in the country of Guinea and winds it way north and east until it runs south through Nigeria. The Niger River forms a large **delta** in southern Nigeria before emptying into the Atlantic Ocean.

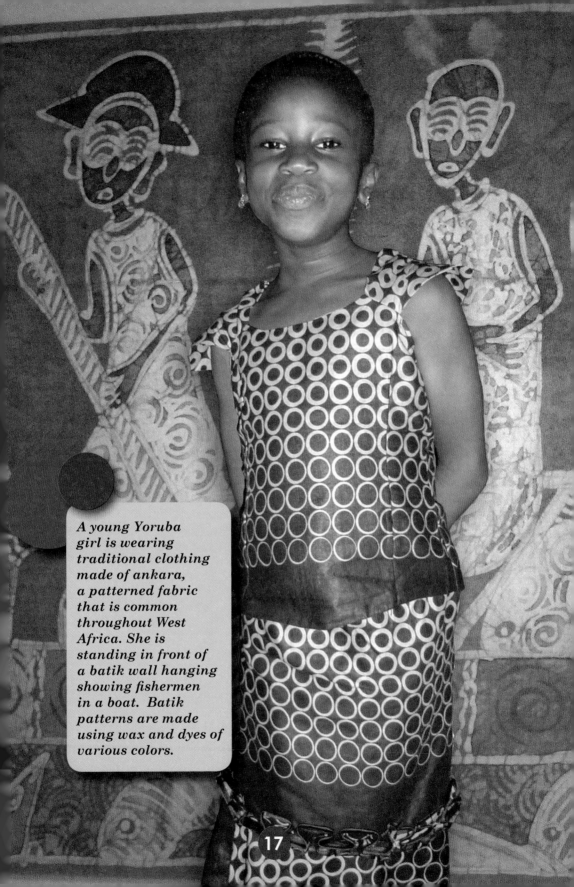

A young Yoruba girl is wearing traditional clothing made of ankara, a patterned fabric that is common throughout West Africa. She is standing in front of a batik wall hanging showing fishermen in a boat. Batik patterns are made using wax and dyes of various colors.

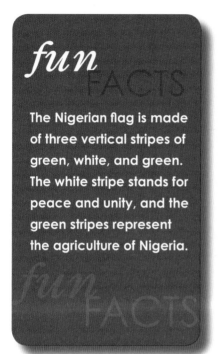

Nigerian flag

The British ruled Nigeria for sixty years, influencing education, politics, language, religion, and nearly every aspect of Nigerian culture. The people of Nigeria did not like being ruled by the British. After a long struggle, Nigeria became an independent nation on October 1, 1960. Since then, Nigerians have elected governments, been ruled by military **dictators,** and even survived a **civil war** in the 1960s. President Umaru Musa Yar'Adua was elected in 2007. Modern Nigeria is made up of 36 states and the federal capital territory of Abuja.

Although Nigeria is the "giant of Africa," it faces some serious challenges. Despite Nigeria's wealth of natural resources, many Nigerians live in poverty. This is partly because some Nigerian leaders have stolen the country's money for themselves. The supply of electricity is not regular, even in large cities. Not all children are

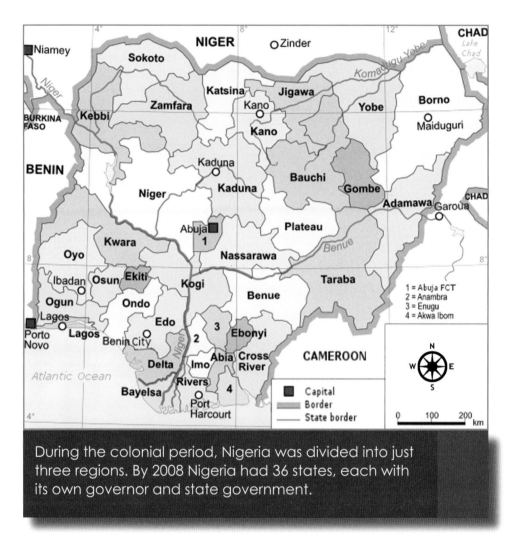

During the colonial period, Nigeria was divided into just three regions. By 2008 Nigeria had 36 states, each with its own governor and state government.

able to attend school, and malaria (mah-LAYR-ee-ah), a disease carried by mosquitoes, causes sickness and death among many children and adults. However, Nigeria's economy is growing, and the people of Nigeria hope that education and hard work will help their country overcome these difficulties.

Nigeria

The baobab tree can grow to almost 100 feet high. Its thick, swollen trunk can store up to 30,000 gallons of water to help it survive during the dry season.

Just North of the Equator

Chapter **3**

The land of Nigeria is as diverse as its people. Covering an area about the size of the states of Oklahoma and Texas combined, Nigeria contains many different climates, landforms, and types of plants. The average daily temperature is about 80 degrees Fahrenheit, but in the north, the temperature can reach as high as 110 degrees Fahrenheit.

There are only two seasons in Nigeria, the dry season (during the winter months) and the wet season (during the summer months). During the winter months, a cold, dry wind from the Sahara called the harmattan reaches even southern Nigeria. The harmattan covers everything with a fine coating of dust.

The Atlantic coast of Nigeria features beaches, marshes, and **lagoons.** The former capital and Nigeria's largest city, Lagos, is located on the southwestern coast. The delta of the Niger River is in the south-central part of the country. This area is very rich in oil. Even though Nigeria earns a great deal of money by selling this oil, the people of the delta are poor and their land has become **polluted.**

A Nigerian mosque is clouded by dust during the harmattan season. Nigerian Muslims worship in mosques on Fridays. Muslims are called to prayer five times each day.

The rain forests of Nigeria lie just north of the coastal region. They receive 60 to 80 inches of rain each year. Palm trees and hardwood trees such as mahogany (mah-HAH-guh-nee) grow here. Many of these forests have been cut down to clear land for farms or to build cities.

The central part of Nigeria is a savanna, or land covered with tall grasses and scattered trees. The distinctive baobab (BAY-oh-bab) and acacia (ah-KAY-shyah) trees grow on the savanna. Crops such as groundnuts (peanuts), **cassava** (kah-SAH-vuh), and millet are grown in this region. Elephants, lions, antelope, and baboons live in this area, but primarily in special game reserves.

In the far northern part of the country is the Sahel, an area that borders the Sahara. This region is very flat, dry, and hot. Only 6 to 20 inches of rain fall there each year. The Sahara creeps farther south each year, a process known as desertification (deh-ZER-tih-fih-KAY-shun).

Cacao seeds

Groundnuts

Cassava

Yams

Grains

Potatoes

Corn

Important crops grown in Nigeria include groundnuts (peanuts), yams, grains, and cassava.

24

The homes in this village found on the Jos Plateau are constructed of traditional materials. The steeply slanted roofs are made of tightly woven palm fronds and the walls are made of hardened earth.

There are mountains in the eastern part of the country, and a large **plateau** near the city of Jos in central Nigeria. The Jos Plateau has many valuable minerals, including tin, iron, coal, gold, and uranium. The climate is somewhat cooler in these areas.

Nigeria

Drums of many different types are played in Nigeria. The most famous Nigerian drum is the "talking drum" (far left and on opposite page). Another popular instrument is the sekere, a gourd covered with beads, shells, or seeds.

Life in
Nigeria

Chapter

4

Nigeria is a land of contrasts. Life in the cities is very different from life in the villages, the customs of each ethnic group are unique, and the modern and the traditional exist side by side.

One of the main differences among the people of Nigeria is religion. Most people who live in northern Nigeria are **Muslims**, and most people who live in southern Nigeria are Christians. About 10 percent of Nigerians practice traditional African religions. The Muslims and the Christians in Nigeria do not always get along with one another. Sometimes there is violence between these two groups.

Nigerian children always wear uniforms to school. After elementary school, students often go to boarding school in a town different from their hometown. (A boarding school provides meals and a place to live for its students.) Classes are taught in English, but students also learn at least one traditional Nigerian language such as Ibo, Hausa, or Yoruba.

Nigerian schoolchildren wear uniforms to school. About 60 percent of Nigerian children attend primary school and about 40 percent attend secondary school.

Nigerian children love to play soccer, anywhere, anytime! The Nigerian national soccer team, the Super Eagles, won the gold medal for men's soccer in the 1996 Olympics. Nigeria is home to many famous soccer players, including Jay-Jay Okocha and Nwankwo Kanu.

Family is very important to Nigerians, and elders are treated with great respect. Children are taught to honor those older than themselves, especially adults. When Yoruba children greet their elders, girls kneel and boys prostrate—or lie facedown—to show respect. Children never call adults by their first names and address them as "ma" or "sir." Most families are large, and extended family members often live together. Muslim men are allowed to have as many as four wives, making some families especially large.

Nigerians do most of their shopping in open-air markets. Supermarkets exist in cities, but most people still go to outdoor markets to buy fresh vegetables, fruits, and meats. There are no prices marked on the goods. The buyer must learn to bargain with the seller to get the best price. Shoppers spend *naira* (NY-rah), the currency of Nigeria.

Soccer is the most popular sport in Nigeria, and many Nigerians play soccer on international (in-ter-NAA-shuh-nul) teams. Children play soccer at home and at school.

Ayo is a popular game of counting and strategy played by both adults and children. Players must "capture" as many seeds as possible while moving their seeds around the board. Rules can be found at www.motherlandnigeria.com/games/ayo.html.

Nigerians celebrate each stage of life with family, friends, and lots of delicious food. For example, Yoruba families hold a naming ceremony eight days after a baby is born. During the ceremony, the family offers special prayers for the newborn child. Other important celebrations include the New Yam Festival in the east, the Argungu Fishing Festival in the north, and various festivals to honor Nigerian gods or ancestors.

These celebrations always include music and dancing. Nigerian music features drums and other percussion instruments. The Yoruba play the "talking drum," a drum that imitates the tones of the Yoruba language. The **sekere** (SHEH-keh-reh), a hollow gourd

The Argungu Fishing Festival takes place each year in the Sokoto River. Fishermen have one hour to catch the largest possible fish using only traditional fishing nets. Fishing is allowed in this spot only once a year during the festival. The largest fish caught in festival history weighed 165 pounds (75 kilograms)!

Yoruba women (above) wearing gele. The gele is a long piece of fabric that is wrapped around the head and shaped into unique styles. For important celebrations, family members usually wear outfits made from identical fabric. Mayowa (below) is dancing with her cousins at a family celebration.

covered with seeds or beads, is another popular musical instrument in Nigeria. Festivals often include dances by groups wearing masks to symbolize ancestors or Nigerian gods.

These celebrations include foods such as **jollof** (joh-LOHF) rice or *eba* (eh-BAH) (cassava) and **egusi** *(eh-GOO-see)* soup. Yams are an important food and are eaten boiled, fried, or pounded. *Dodo*, or fried plantain, is a favorite food for young and old alike. Most Nigerian food contains red pepper, tomatoes, and onions, and is very spicy!

Traditional Nigerian clothing is flowing and colorful. Women wear skirts of brightly colored fabrics wrapped around their waists, matching blouses, and head-scarves. Yoruba women are known for their elaborate headscarves called **gele** (GAY-lay). Men wear loose robes of cotton with embroidered patterns. Families often wear outfits of matching fabrics when attending a celebration.

Nigerian Authors

Nigerian authors have continued the ancient tradition of storytelling. Ibo author Chinua Achebe wrote the novel *Things Fall Apart*, about the arrival of the white man in Ibo land. Students around the world study this book in school. Yoruba author Wole Soyinka won the Nobel Prize for Literature in 1986. He was the first black African to win this prize. Mr. Soyinka has written many plays, poems, and novels about Nigerian life.

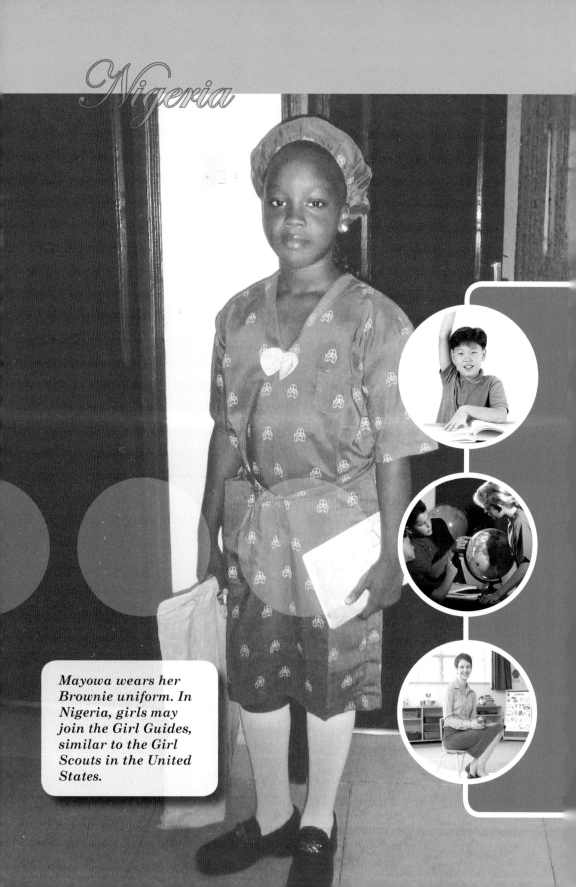

Mayowa wears her Brownie uniform. In Nigeria, girls may join the Girl Guides, similar to the Girl Scouts in the United States.

Kaabo, Mayowa!

Chapter **5**

Julie and her classmates had done their homework and were ready to welcome Mayowa to their classroom. They had made a bulletin board about Nigeria and a banner that read, *Kaabo, Mayowa!* Mayowa's family is Yoruba, and the word for "welcome" in Yoruba is **kaabo** (KAH-ah-boh). Julie and her friends had practiced pronouncing this word and a few others:

English	Yoruba
Good morning	*Kaaro* (KAH-ah-roh)
Goodbye	*O dabo* (oh DAH-boh)
Thank you	*E se* (eh shay)
Yes	*Beni* (BEH-nee)
No	*Oti* (OH-tee)

Mrs. Harkins and the students had prepared *dodo*, and everyone in the class was eager to try it. They had made masks out of brown paper bags and decorated them with Yoruba designs they'd found on the Internet.

Mayowa entered the classroom wearing a heavy sweater. She was not used to the chilly fall weather of Newark, Delaware. Julie and her classmates shouted, "*Kaabo*, Mayowa! Welcome to Delaware!" Mayowa's face lit up, and she smiled at Mrs. Harkins and her new classmates.

"Thank you so much! How did you know how to greet me in my language? Oh, a map of Nigeria and a flag, too! Is that *dodo* on the table? It's my favorite food!"

Julie and her classmates crowded around Mayowa and asked her questions about Nigeria. Mayowa showed them pictures of her home in Lagos and her family.

"Is this your sister, Mayowa?" asked Julie.

"Yes, this is Sister Tolu [TOH-loo], and Mama and Papa," answered Mayowa. "Here is a picture of our house in Lagos. In Nigeria, houses are made of cement blocks, to help keep the house cool."

"Does our school look like your school in Lagos?" asked Mrs. Harkins.

"No, ma," answered Mayowa. "The playground here is larger than the one in Lagos, and children always wear uniforms to school in Nigeria."

Seun Adewale, Mayowa's father; Bimbola Adewale, Mayowa's mother; Tolu Adewale, Mayowa's older sister; and Mayowa outside their home in Lagos.

This ivory mask was made in the 1500s to honor the mother of the oba, or king, of the Benin Empire.

Like other Nigerian homes in cities, Mayowa's house is made of concrete and includes a wall around the yard (called a compound) and a small shop off to the side.

"Why did your family move to Delaware, Mayowa?" asked Eric.

"My father is studying electrical engineering at the university," said Mayowa. "He works for the power company in Lagos. We plan to return to Nigeria after Papa earns his degree."

On the playground, Mayowa and Julie discovered that they played many of the same games. In Lagos, hopscotch is called *suwe* (SOO-way), hide and seek is called *boju boju* (BOH-joo BOH-joo), and a game like rock, paper, scissors is called *ten ten*.

Like children everywhere, Nigerian young people love to play. With or without fancy equipment, Nigerian children enjoy recess.

At the end of the day, Julie realized that she had much in common with Mayowa. They both loved to play soccer and to cook. Mayowa promised to teach Julie some new soccer moves, and Julie promised to teach Mayowa how to bake brownies. Julie also realized that she had just begun to learn about the wonderful nation of Nigeria. She already had a new set of questions to ask Mayowa in the morning!

The plantain is a relative of the banana. Plantains can be purchased in large supermarkets or in Hispanic grocery stores. They are ripe when they are somewhat soft and are yellow with black or brown marks.

How To Make
Dodo
(Fried Plantain)

Recipe

You Will Need

An adult to help you

Table Knife

Cutting Board

Frying Pan

Spatula

Paper Towels

Serving Platter

Ingredients

2 or 3 ripe plantains

Cooking oil

Instructions

1. Use a table knife to peel the plantain. Cut it into diagonal slices about one inch thick.

2. **Ask an adult** to heat about 1 inch of cooking oil in a heavy frying pan.

3. With the adult's help, carefully place the plantain slices in the hot oil. Fry over medium heat for about 2 minutes on each side, or until golden brown.

4. Remove the pieces from the pan and place them on paper towels to soak up any extra oil.

5. Serve warm.

Make Your Own
Nigerian Mask

You Will Need

An adult to help you

Large brown paper grocery bags

Scissors

Markers

Masks are often worn by dancers in festivals to represent ancestors or Nigerian gods. These dances are called masquerades. Designs for masks can be found on the Internet or in books of African art. You might check out these sites: Printable African Masks for Kids to Color (http://www.scissorcraft.com/masks.htm) and National Museum of African Art: Design or Draw a Mask (http://africa.si.edu/exhibits/playful/behindindex.html).

Instructions for Making a Nigerian Mask

1 Ask an adult to place a large brown paper bag loosely over your head, then carefully mark openings for your eyes.

2 Lay the bag flat on a table and decorate. You can make your own designs, or copy one from a book or Internet site (see top of page).

3 Cut out the openings for the eyes. If you wish, you can decorate your mask further by cutting a fringe on the bottom.

Further Reading

Books

Blauer, Ettagale, and Jason Lauré. *Nigeria*. New York: Children's Press, 2001.

Bowden, Rob, and Roy Maconachie. *The Changing Face of Nigeria*. Chicago: Raintree, 2004.

Freville, Nicholas. *Nigeria*. Philadelphia: Chelsea House Publishers, 2000.

Giles, Bridget. *Nigeria*. Washington, D.C.: National Geographic, 2007.

Hamilton, Janice. *Nigeria in Pictures*. Minneapolis: Lerner Publications, 2003.

Harmon, Daniel. *Nigeria*. Philadelphia: Chelsea House Publishers, 2001.

Nnoromele, Salome. *Nigeria*. San Diego: Lucent Books, 2002.

Nigerian Tales

Anderson/Sankofa, David. *The Origin of Life on Earth*. Mt. Airy, Maryland: Sight Productions, 1991.

Arnott, Kathleen. *Tales From Africa*. New York: Oxford University Press, 2000.

Bartók, Mira. *Stencils—West Africa: Nigeria*. Glenview, Illinois: Good Year Books, 1994.

Echewa, T. Obinkaram. *The Magic Tree: A Tale from Nigeria*. New York: Morrow Junior Books, 1999.

Onyefulu, Ifeoma. *Chidi Only Likes Blue*. New York: Cobblehill Books,1997.

————. *Ogbo: Sharing Life in an African Village*. San Diego: Gulliver Books, 1996.

Works Consulted

This book is based on author Anna Ogunnaike's personal experiences living in Nigeria and being part of a Nigerian family. The author also consulted with Nigerian friends and relatives. Other works consulted are listed below.

BBC Country Profile: *Nigeria*
http://news.bbc.co.uk/1/hi/world/africa/country_profiles/1064557.stm

Holmes, Peter. *Nigeria: Giant of Africa*. London: Swallow Editions Ltd., 1987.

O'Neill, Tom. "Curse of the Black Gold." *National Geographic*. February 2007, pp. 88–117.

Ogunnaike, Babatunde. Personal interview on life in Nigeria. Hockessin, Delaware. January 12, 2008.

Olu-Lafe, Oluyomi. Personal interview on Nigerian children's games. Stevens Point, Wisconsin. January 21, 2008.

Soyinka, Wole. *The Open Sore of a Continent*. New York: Oxford University Press, 1996.

Further Reading

The Library of Congress. *A Country Study: Nigeria*
　　http://memory.loc.gov/frd/cs/ngtoc.html
Zwingle, Erla. "Megacities." *National Geographic*. November 2002, pp.
　　70–99.

On the Internet
Motherland Nigeria: Kidzone
　　http://www.motherlandnigeria.com/kidzone.html
National Anthem of Nigeria(download both the music and the lyrics)
　　http://www.nationalanthems.info/ng-78.htm
　　http://www.nationalanthems.info/ng.htm
PBS: Independent Lens: Nigerian Music (hear famous Nigerian musicians)
　　http://www.pbs.org/independentlens/newamericans/culturalriches/
　　music_nigerian.html
"This Is Nigeria," Embassy of the Federal Republic of Nigeria
　　http://www.nigeriaembassyusa.org/thisisnigeria.shtml

Embassy
Embassy of the Federal Republic of Nigeria
3519 International Court, NW
Washington, DC 20008
Tel: (202) 986-8400
Fax: (202) 775-1385
http://www.nigeriaembassyusa.org/f_index.html

Naira—
Nigerian
money

Glossary

Italics indicate a Yoruba word

archaeologist (ar-kee-AH-luh-jist)—A person who studies the way people lived long ago by digging up the remains of ancient cities and towns.

caravan (KAYR-uh-van)—A group of people who travel together.

cassava (kah-SAH-vah)—A starchy root plant, the source of tapioca (taa-pee-OH-kuh).

city-state—A region controlled by a city.

civilization (sih-vih-lih-ZAY-shun)—A society in which trade, agriculture, and science are developed.

civil war (SIH-vul WAR)—A war fought between citizens of one country.

colony (KAH-luh-nee)—A territory ruled by another country.

delta—An area of land at the mouth of a river, formed by deposits of mud.

dictator (DIK-tay-tur)—An unelected ruler with absolute power.

ebony (EH-buh-nee)—A hard, black wood.

egusi (eh-GOO-see)—Melon seed that is ground up and used in Nigerian cooking.

equator (ee-KWAY-tur)—An imaginary line around the middle of the earth, halfway between the North and South Poles.

gele (GAY-lay)—Fancy Yoruba headdress for women.

Islam (IZ-lahm)—The religion of the Muslims that teaches there is one God, Allah, and that Muhammad was his prophet.

ivory (YV-ree)—A smooth, white substance that forms the tusks of elephants.

jollof (joh-LOHF) **rice**—Traditional Nigerian rice dish cooked with tomatoes, peppers, spices, and meat.

kaabo (KAH-ah-boh)—Yoruba word for "welcome."

lagoon (luh-GOON)—A shallow body of water usually connected to a larger body of water.

Muslim (MUZ-lim)—A person who practices the religion of Islam.

nomadic (noh-MAD-ik)—Wandering from place to place to follow good weather or hunting grounds; not having a permanent home.

plantation (plan-TAY-shun)—A large estate or farm, usually that grows one type of crop.

plateau (plah-TOH)—High, flat land.

polluted (puh-LOO-ted)—Dirty.

populous (PAH-pyoo-lus)—Having many people.

sekere (SHEH-keh-reh)—Nigerian musical instrument made of a hollow gourd covered with beads.

terra-cotta (tayr-uh-KAH-tuh)—Hard, brownish red clay.

Index

ABOUT THE AUTHOR

Anna M. Ogunnaike, a teacher and home-educator, lives in Hockessin, Delaware, with her husband and their three sons. Anna is a graduate of the University of Wisconsin-Madison and the University of Lagos. An American by birth, Anna lived in Oshodi, Lagos, Nigeria, from 1983 to 1988 and has been part of a wonderful, extended Nigerian family since her marriage to Dr. Babatunde Ogunnaike in 1983.

The Ogunnaike family (left to right): Deji, Babatunde, Anna, Damini, and Makinde (front)